MADE-UP HOLIDAYS COLLECTION

CONNOR WHITELEY

No part of this book may be reproduced in any form or by any electronic or mechanical means. Including information storage, and retrieval systems, without written permission from the author except for the use of brief quotations in a book review.

This book is NOT legal, professional, medical, financial or any type of official advice.

Any questions about the book, rights licensing, or to contact the author, please email connorwhiteley@connorwhiteley.net

Copyright © 2023 CONNOR WHITELEY

All rights reserved.

DEDICATION
Thank you to all my readers without you I couldn't do what I love.

INTRODUCTION

When it comes to the holiday season, people always talk about the magic, food and presents. Then they may eventually start talking about the little traditions each of us have and what makes the holiday season so special to each of us.

I know me and my best friends back in school would always use the last week before the Christmas break to tell each other about how Christmas worked for us. Since each family had their own special traditions and little things that made the season their own.

I bet you have some too.

So in this collection based on the Holiday Extravaganza 2022 I wanted to bring together and write a bunch of stories that focus on the little Made-Up holidays that can make the holiday season even more special to some people.

Sometimes these Made-Up holidays involve lone criminals wanting to steal something. Other times it's gripping private eyes wanting to celebrate with their friends or save a street's happiness. And other times it is fantastical witches and wizards wanting to inspire and surprise us with their Made-Up Holidays.

Whether you're more of a mystery or fantasy fan, these wonderful enthralling Holiday stories are sure to provide the perfect escape at any time of the year but most importantly, during the strangely stressful and chaotic time of the Holiday season.

Enjoy!

AUTHOR OF BETTIE ENGLISH PRIVATE EYE MYSTERIES

CONNOR WHITELEY

PROTECTING CHRISTMAS
A HOLIDAY MYSTERY CRIME SHORT STORY

INTRODUCTION
Mood/ Genre: Light Crime

If you thought you were only going to get wonderfully light goody-two-shoe stories from me then I hate (not) to tell you, you are sadly mistaken.

But don't worry because today we have a great light crime short story as it is National Package Protection Day.

When I first heard of this made-up holiday, my mind immediately went to two different places on the mystery fiction spectrum. I was tempted to write a Bettie Private Eye short story set today, but then I realised I ready had a few of them lined up for the Holiday Extravaganza.

Thankfully my mind went somewhere else too, it went to the criminal side. Because surely the packages need to be protected from something?

Cue criminals!

But our next story is filled with twists and surprises, so if you think this is your normal theft

short story, think again!
 Enjoy!

PROTECTING CHRISTMAS

National Parcel Protection Day (in the US at least) had to be the greatest of Holidays to Jessica, it was a day basically begging for crime to be committed, parcels stolen and their protectors in tears over their failures.

And Jessica was only too happy to oblige.

Jessica wasn't a bad person, she didn't steal for herself, she didn't steal for thrills or any of those so-called excuses, she stole for the good of others.

That reason was a simple excuse according to many of her friends but Jessica loved the holiday season and National Parcel Protection Day most of all, it was her way of giving back.

As Jessica stood in the wonderful little street with small houses packed together with a (rather pathetic) little road separating them, Jessica felt the excitement filling her as she prepared for her first steal of the day.

The air smelt wonderfully of warming Christmas spices, one of the houses were probably baking some mince pies, a little early but each to their own, and Jessica loved the sound of the children singing (badly) at school a few blocks away.

Jessica wasn't sure if she liked the neighbourhood or houses along the street too much. Sure they had Christmas decorations, lights and wreaths hanging all over them. But there was something strange about them, they were all the same, identical and not in a beautiful way.

The bitter cold was another reason Jessica didn't like the neighbourhood, every neighbourhood in England had a certain (extremely varying) degree of charm to it and even the houses that were meant to look alike had their own faults and aspects of character to it.

These houses did not.

If Jessica was to guess, she might have believed some American developer had created this street or something but she didn't know. And she most certainly didn't want to find out. This street felt weird.

The wonderfully spice scented air got stronger and Jessica licked her lips as she imagined their amazing fruity, spicy taste in her mouth. Maybe she would have to steal some for herself.

Jessica hated that idea. That was flat out wrong, stealing for oneself was never good and Jessica had learnt that first hand as a child.

As a homeless child living, eating and stealing on the streets, she had to get food somehow but she stole from the wrong baker one day, and ended by getting beaten within an inch of her life because of it.

When she recovered, got a job a few years later

and learnt that her true family had died in a car crash and left her some money, Jessica vowed to help those on the streets like no one had ever done for her.

The sound of the children singing started to die down as the howl of the bitter wind grew. That was probably the worse thing about the streets, their cold unloving nature. Maybe she would buy some thick coats for the homeless with the money she got from today's theft.

The sound of a large white van driving slowly down the street made Jessica stare at it. Jessica wasn't a fan of white vans, they reminded her too much of scary child kidnapping films and there was something about the speed of the van.

The van shouldn't have been driving that slowly, the entire street was perfectly clean of cars, so the van was hardly going to bump into anything.

Jessica stepped back a little and focused on the drivers. There was one man wearing a black tracksuit and a black cap covering most of his face, and a tall woman was wearing a long black coat.

But what Jessica didn't like was how they were looking each house up and down and around.

That look was all too familiar to Jessica, she had given the entire road those looks twice today already. She had calculated from a bit of research that the post people always come at 12 o'clock on this road like clockwork.

It was almost time and all the houses in the road were empty.

Jessica wasn't sure what the people in the van were doing but she didn't like it. She wanted to go over there, pound on the window and get them to go. This was her road to steal from and at least she was going to give her stolen items to a good cause.

These people weren't, Jessica had run into these sorts of people before. White van drivers that were thieves were never good people to get involved with.

If she could just get one parcel without those people seeing her, then she could get something for the homeless people.

The sound of the van doors slamming shut made Jessica's eyes widen as she saw the man and woman leant against the van and stare at her.

Jessica didn't know what to do. She could run, but she didn't want to be chased.

"You wanna parcel?" the man asked.

Jessica was surprised by his deep, disease ridden voice. He definitely wasn't the healthiest man she had ever met, but there was something creepy about him. The way he stared at her and bit his lip.

"Ah come on Luv," the man said, gesturing her to come close.

Jessica wasn't sure why they were here. If the man and woman had been here for parcels then they should have waited in the van, seen the post people leave the parcels and then steal them.

But they wanted Jessica to come closer to them.

She didn't like this one bit.

"I've got some presents in my van ya can have,"

the man said.

Jessica's mouth dropped. This man and woman were foul people, they wanted to kidnap her. Jessica was shocked. How dare they come to this street, on her favourite National Day and try to pull a stunt like this.

The sound of children cheering echoed around the neighbour from the school.

"Leave!" Jessica shouted.

She wasn't going to let them kidnap a child if that was their plan, if the local school was finishing earlier today then Jessica was never going to let one of the children anywhere near these people.

Jessica had almost been stolen herself on the streets before, she was never ever going to let another child experience that!

"We ain't doing anything wrong. We just waiting outside out van," the woman said.

Jessica sneered at them both. "What's your plan then? Steal a few children. Get their parents to pay you. Then have a merry Christmas,"

The man and woman smiled at each other.

"What is it to ya?" the man asked.

"I will not let you steal children on my day!"

The man laughed. "Ya Day? What are ya the Queen?"

Queen Jessica, it did have a nice ring to it. But as much as Jessica loved that idea, she had to try to do something today of all days. The holiday was meant to be about Protection after all.

"Go now or I *will* call the police," Jessica said.

The man mockingly cried. "Ya really think ta police will show up for two peeps leaning against a van,"

Jessica wanted to protest but that was a harsh truth about the world they lived in. Years of cut backs, politics and everything had left all public services decimated to varying degrees, the police was no less affected than any other public service.

After spending about ten years as a police call handler Jessica remembered that all too well.

"Tell ya what luv. Leave. We let you live," the man said.

Jessica shook her head. "I am not leaving you two alone,"

"Come on, you must have some fam. Ready want 'em to receive your ransom?" the woman said.

Jessica was glad she didn't have any still alive. She hated her true family for abandoning her and when they died it was almost joyous to her. But how dare these idiots threaten her, they were going to be in for a hell of a surprise. She had lived on the streets long enough to learn how to defend herself.

The amazing smell of warm mince pies made Jessica realise there had to be someone at home in one of the houses, maybe if she was loud enough they would check on the situation.

But what would it look like?

She wasn't sure. All it probably looked like were two strange people leaning against a van and a crazy woman who clearly wasn't from the neighbourhood shouting at them.

"My family wouldn't pay for pay anyway," Jessica said.

The man grabbed his genitals. "I would luv,"

That was the final straw, Jessica had to do something. This man was disgusting and it was even more disgusting that this lady friend (girlfriend, wife, mistress?) wasn't saying anything.

Then Jessica remembered how cruel both men and women can be to homeless children on the street.

Jessica looked at her watch. It was a few minutes to twelve. The post people would be here soon, maybe that could save her and the children.

"You need to go now!" Jessica shouted, tapping her watch.

The man grinned. "Ya think ta postman is gonna stop us. We'll just gut him, like we will ya!"

The man whipped out a knife.

The woman did the same.

Jessica froze.

They both ran at her.

Her street training kicked in.

The man swung.

Jessica ducked.

Slamming her fists into his jaw.

He moaned.

Jessica kicked the woman in the chest.

She screamed.

The man swung again.

Quickly.

There were too many strikes coming.

Jessica ducked.

She rolled.

She jumped up.

Smashing her fists into the man's spine.

Something cracked.

The woman swung.

Jessica punched her.

The knife almost cutting her.

The woman jumped forward.

Knocking Jessica to the ground.

The knife sliced her.

The woman attacked again.

Thrusting the knife into Jessica's chest.

She screamed.

Jessica grabbed the woman's hands.

Forcing the knife to remain in her.

The woman looked scared.

Jessica headbutted her.

She let go of the knife.

Jessica whacked the woman.

She fell to the ground.

Jessica stomped on her head.

The man got up.

Jessica kicked him in the head.

Jessica frowned at the man and woman on the ground with blood on their face and a wave of discomfort washed over Jessica as she feared they were dead. She never wanted to kill them.

Jessica checked their pulses.

To her relief both the man and the woman were unconscious and not dead. A very small part of her wanted them dead, at least that way they wouldn't be able to hurt any more children ever again.

But the truth for Jessica was she wasn't a killer. Even during her darkest days on the streets, she never hurt anyone who didn't deserve it.

She bit her lip as a wave of pain from the stab wound washed over her. Jessica pressed the wound gently and she was relieved that it wasn't bleeding, it wasn't a bad cut and at least she would still be around to help the homeless.

The sound of police sirens in the distance was almost angelic to Jessica as that had to be a sign that the children would be safe and these two would be sent to prison. At least she had somehow honoured her favourite National Day, whilst she didn't have any presents for the homeless people today, at least she had protected the innocent from these idiots.

And that was a good day in her books.

The sound of the police sirens were getting closer so Jessica went up to the back of the white van, kicked the lock and opened it for the police.

Jessica was shocked at all the rope, candies and comic books that the two creeps had both for the children. She was more than glad she had stopped them now and at least the police could clearly see that the man and woman were the bad guys, and not her.

As Jessica walked off into the distance leaving

the police to find the man, woman and the incriminating white van, Jessica was filled with delight that her National Parcel Day had gone so perfectly.

She was going to remember this for a long, long time.

MADE-UP HOLIDAYS COLLECTION

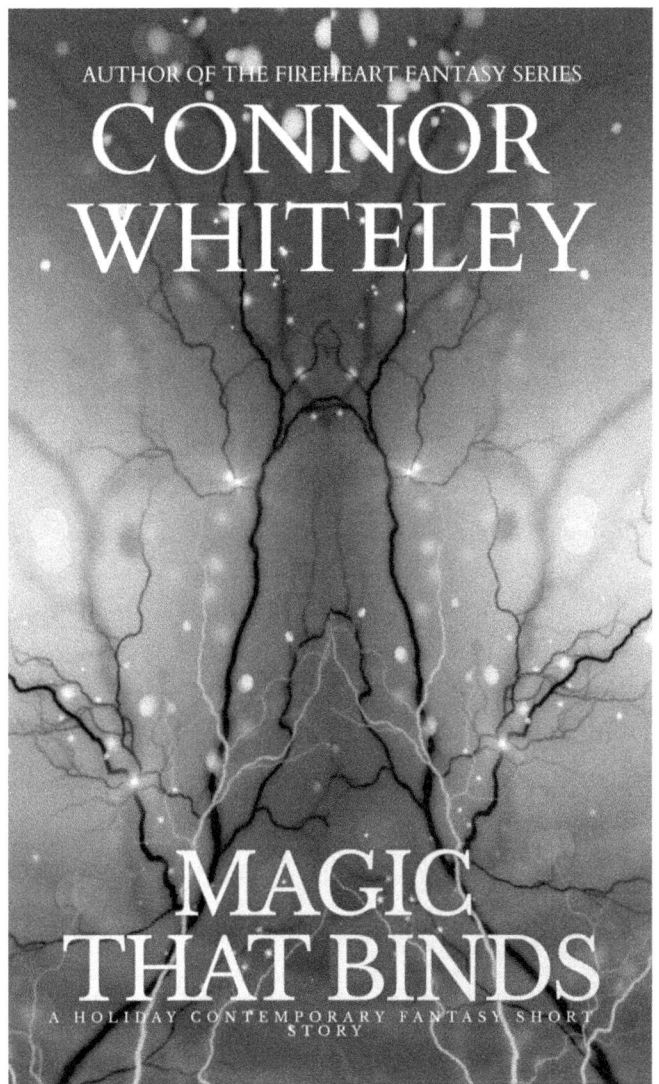

Introduction

Mood/ Genre: Light Contemporary Fantasy

Today's holiday short story is another one that is rather different compared to what I normally write, but in a good way of course.

There isn't really too much I can say about this light fantasy story, because the story really does speak for itself.

However, what I can say is today is what's known as Make A Gift day, so I immediately jumped to the fantasy genre to create a story inspired by the spirit of this made-up holiday.

So please check out this wonderful fantasy story about freedom, magic and gift-giving.

Enjoy!

MADE-UP HOLIDAYS COLLECTION

MAGIC THAT BINDS

It might have started off as a hobby but to Janet making gifts was all part of the holiday season experience. It was amazing, wonderful to make people such wondrous gifts, Janet was known to everyone in Kent, England as the best gift maker because of her ability to infuse even the most hideous objects with her magic and make them stunning.

Janet stood in a smaller isle in a massive craft superstore surrounded by rows upon rows of beads in all their different sizes, textures and colours.

Beads might have been awful, small and annoying to some people, but to Janet they were magical things that were the best material to make gifts from. Their small round size meant it didn't take much magic to manipulate them into whatever shape she wanted.

And as a part-time teacher at the local sixth form for young magic users, the beads were perfect to allow them to experiment with their magic.

She had stopped using wooden and other large material a long time ago, young inexperienced magic users definitely shouldn't unleash the magical energy needed to manipulate large pieces of wood until they were ready.

Janet hated to think about all the fires, explosions and other accidents caused by them.

But beads were perfect.

The smell of the little plastic beads wasn't the best but when mixed together with flowers, natural materials and maybe even a hint of lavender, these beads would smell amazing, and that was what Janet loved about gift making.

The sound of other customers and their children in the other isles reminded Janet of her own love of the different crafts. She loved the bright lively strokes of painting and the wonderful hands-on nature of pottery.

But the containers of bright red, blue and green beads in front of her head were what Janet needed at this point in time. Maybe she could check out the paints and pottery bits later. Perhaps even her husband could buy her a few pieces for Christmas.

Janet placed her hands into the containers of the plastic beads. Their icy coldness felt amazing, their smooth cold texture was a stunning, beautiful contrast to her aged rough hands.

But she needed to find magic sensitive beads.

These types of beads were often made by magic users in the factories and mixed in with the rest of the beads to stop them from being detected (Not everyone was as respectable towards magic users as they should have been), but Janet had detected a strong number of the magical beads in this aisle alone.

That was unusual yet that was the last thing on Janet's priorities at the moment as her annoying (but wonderfully rich) client had given her an awful deadline to make a gift by the end of the day.

Janet didn't like to rush gifts. Each one was carefully planned, made and delivered. Each one took at least three days to make so making a wonderful gift in a single day was going to be difficult. Not impossible. Just difficult.

The only solace Janet could take from the impossible request was the amazing contract and payday that came with it. Ten thousand pounds for the gift and the exclusive contract of being the client's personal gift maker.

Normally that wouldn't interest Janet, but considering the client was a rich businessman who entertained hundreds of clients every year in London. The pay checks would be like shooting fish in a barrel.

Janet finished searching the containers in front of her head and frowned.

This was silly. She had detected the magic here and now they were gone. She was running out of time. Janet had to create this gift in time.

Janet closed her eyes and called on her powers, she used them to sense and search through the containers, if the beads were here then her magic should be able to find them.

Nothing. Except the moderately strong remains of their magical signatures.

Janet hated that the beads had been so close but she was too late to get them. Perhaps she could go and search the store and maybe the car park, then buy them off the person who had them, but Janet wasn't sure in the slightest.

"Mrs Janet Oblong?" an elderly lady said.

Janet looked at the tall elderly lady with her purple power suit, long brown hair and perfectly aged face. Janet couldn't understand how the woman could sound like a ninety-year-old but look not a day over thirty.

Well, she could. The woman had to be a fellow magic user.

"How do you know my name?" Janet asked.

The woman smiled. "I am Lady Michelle, and I know a lot about you,"

Janet didn't believe her in the slightest.

"Janet Oblong grew up in Canterbury England and went to university at The University of Magic in the city for five years, completing a degree in Psychology specialising in Magical Mental Health and then doing another degree in Magical Studies,"

Janet was impressed but surely this woman could have found all that out online. Maybe this Lady was a creepy stalker or something.

"I'm not a stalker, Janet,"

Janet's eyes widened.

"And before you think it, I am a telepath. That is

my main discipline. My husband Lord Michelle is a lot better at it but I manage,"

Janet wanted to wonder who the hell this woman was, but she didn't, she couldn't have this Lady Michelle reading her thoughts. So she fell back on her training and what her degree had taught her to do.

Simply don't think about anything important.

"Clever Janet. I wasn't sure if you remembered your training,"

Janet stepped forward. "Do I know you?"

"In a way. I always watched your classes. Loved University myself. But I was always at the edges of everyone's mind,"

Janet took a step back. "Who the hell are you?"

"You seek beads to make a gift. I have beads and want a gift,"

Janet didn't even care if the woman read her mind anymore. This was just strange and crazy, the Lady Michelle was clearly a stalker of some kind. It wasn't natural for a telepath or any magic user to watch university students and read the thoughts at the edge of their minds.

It was probably the weirdest thing Janet had ever heard of.

"Oh now Janet, I have heard of stranger things. Me brushing past the edges of your mind isn't strange. It's comforting. I'm a guardian of sorts,"

Janet just wanted those beads and to go home. She didn't have time for this Lady Michelle, or whatever the hell she was.

"A Guardian?" Janet asked, her voice unsure.

"Yes dear Janet. I used to work for the University's Mental Health Services and I spent my day brushing through the minds of the students checking on their wellbeing,"

"You're lying. You didn't check on their wellbeing. You invaded their privacy, and doesn't magical law prohibit you searching the minds of others?"

Lady Michelle laughed hard. "Dearest Janet, the Law is old and outdated. I might have scarred myself by looking through the thoughts of the students, and believe me it's… interesting what some people get up to. But I saved lives,"

Janet realised this woman certainly wasn't normal, but she felt like a woman with a purpose. This was no chance meeting or simply seeing Janet and wanting to talk. Lady Michelle had planned to meet her and make Janet talk to her.

"My client's your husband, isn't he?" Janet asked.

Lady Michelle nodded. "Clever girl. Sure, my husband doesn't know I am here but still. He wants the gift for me and I want something from you in return,"

"What?" Janet asked, checking for the nearest escape route.

"I want you to work for me,"

Janet's eyes narrowed. "Work for you? I don't even know what you do,"

A family of small children and two parents

walked into the aisle and Lady Michelle gestured Janet to walk with her.

It was hard to keep up with Lady Michelle's long legs but Janet managed.

"Me and my Husband might be members of the English Nobility but we have a side business too,"

Whatever it was Janet didn't want any part in it. From her years of experience, all side businesses were criminal and dodgy as any criminal gang. Hell, most the side businesses Janet had dealt with were ran by criminals.

She had to get the beads and escape.

"We are not criminals Janet,"

Damn! Janet had forgotten about the telepath thing. She had to remain focused and forget her thoughts.

"What is this side business?" Janet asked.

Lady Michelle looked around. "Coast is clear. You know the Anti-Supernatural Bill going through the Houses of Parliament and Lords at the moment,"

Janet couldn't believe she would even mention such an outrageous thing in a public place. The Bill, Act or whatever else the UK government decided to call it would ruin her and her business.

All Janet wanted was to make jewellery, sell it and give people joy in their lives. She wasn't going to hurt anyone, but just because a gang of five magic users decided to go round killing people, the UK Government saw its chance to make magic illegal.

It was wrong!

Janet had wanted to move to Scotland more times than she cared to admit because their leaders seemed to like Magic Users. But it didn't matter in the end, if the UK Government made magic illegal then it would find a way to make Scotland make it illegal too.

The wonders of UK politics!

Janet frowned. "What about it?"

Lady Michelle looked around again. "Me and my husband are the only Magic Users in UK politics. The Bill will pass and our people will be doomed,"

Janet wanted to leave now. It would be Christmas in a few weeks, all she wanted to do was make her gifts and get on with her life. She didn't want to think about this.

"The Bill will be passed before Christmas," Lady Michelle said.

"Why tell me this? I am a simple Gift Maker,"

Lady Michelle smiled. "That is why I sought you out. Ever since I first met... brush your mind at university I knew you were different. You love the world, you love magic, you love your creations. I do not believe you want that to end on your watch,"

Janet hated when other people were right. Especially this Lady Michelle, Janet loved creating gifts, spreading the joy and showing others the wonders of magic. She didn't want to stop, she wasn't going to stop, no matter what the Law was.

Lady Michelle knelt in front of Janet. "I am begging you Janet Oblong to help me,"

The sight of a Lady kneeling on the ground and

getting dust and dirt all over her power suit was something, and Janet realised that these words weren't the act of a malice or manipulative woman.

These were the words of a scared woman who just wanted to do the best for her people.

"Rise Lady Michelle," Janet said, always wanting to say that. "What must I do?"

Lady Michelle got the beads out of her pocket.

"I need you to make a gift. I need you to make a gift that is so great for all 600 members of Parliament. Show the Elected Officials of the UK what magic can offer. Prove to them the power of magic and how joyous it is and show them how magic binds us all together,"

"What about the Lords?" Janet asked.

Lady Michelle smiled. "You deal with the Elected Officials. I will deal with the Lords personally,"

Janet took the beads from Lady Michelle, rushed back home and got to work on the gifts.

Time was running out for her kind.

***

Janet sat in front of her massive TV with her beautiful husband next to her as she watched all the Elected Officials of the UK Government vote on the Anti-Magic Bill.

Her small living room smelt of the lavender, scented oils and oranges that she had used to make all the gifts and now she hoped that her hard work had been enough.

She had made every one of them the best gift she

could and Janet just hoped it was enough to make them support magic.

According to the News, this was the first time ever in Parliament's history that every single member had been present to take part in a vote. Normally that would have concerned her, but tonight she couldn't care less.

Janet gripped her husband's magically charged hands tighter as a tall man stood up on the television and read out the results.

Her heart was thumping in her chest as the next few seconds would determine her life, her husband's life and the life of her people.

"The Yeses have 2 Votes. The Noes have 598 Votes. The Noes have it. The Noes have it!"

Janet felt an immense wave of relaxation wash over her, but the sound from the television was deafening as every single (minus the two that voted yes) Elected Official jumped up and celebrated.

No one wanted magic to be outlawed.

And it was all because of Janet. Sure no one would ever know how she had saved magic, but Janet didn't care. She only cared about the making of her gifts, sharing the joy and most importantly showing people how magic binds everyone together in joy.

Whatever tomorrow was going to bring, Janet looked forward to it because she had saved magic, got the contract with Lord Michelle and now she was even helping Lady Michelle sell her gifts internationally as part of her side business.

But all that could wait.

Because tonight Janet was going to celebrate with the man she loved, and there was nothing that was going to stop her as she took him off to the bedroom for a long amazing night.

INTRODUCTION

Genre/ Mood: Light Crime With Romantic Elements

Enough with all this goody too shoes rubbish about the holiday season, the month of December isn't all about goodness, light and the family.

Sometimes it's about darker topics, like theft, crime and stealing, because this is a wonderful time of year for the darker side of humanity to show itself.

And that is what we have in the next story in the Holiday Extravaganza as we celebrate National Letter Writing Day in a wonderful criminal style.

You'll enjoy this one!

CHRISTMAS, CRIME, LETTER

Elizabeth State was dead, but now she lives again.

Of course she wasn't really, that would just be silly. But in a strange way she was alive once more through me, as it was her identity that my guy gave me for tonight's rather… lavish party and my theft.

I stood in the massive white room with walls reaching high into the sky and stretching as far back as I could see, and in the middle of the room there was a rather… interesting (tasteless) column with two sets of stone stairs spiralling around that, leading to two exhibition rooms.

My targets.

Now I called this the opening area of the British Museum (there probably was an official name but I didn't care).

If I was alone in here then I would definitely have taken advantage, stealing from the food court that was on the far, far side of the room and maybe even stealing from the gift shop that was rumoured to be around here.

But sadly I wasn't.

I was surrounded by the snobs of the almighty rich and powerful of the Museum's largest donors, and when I mean largest I do mean it. I don't know how some of these donors would fit on their private jets or even get into buildings. They were walking, talking, smelly tanks.

Thankfully they were some thinner donors too!

Yet I must admit watching most of these stunning fit rich men in their tight black suits, smooth faces and expensive haircuts, it was almost enough to make a woman fluster and turn red.

But I am nothing short of professional. I am here to do a theft after all.

I grabbed a glass of golden champagne and circulated through the crowd, since the most amateur mistake you can make is to survey the entire room from one spot. That's what all the security guards watch for.

The sounds of the rich men and women talking, laughing and snorting filled my ears as I circulated the room. Looking out for security guards, undercovers and any more surprises.

Now my theft was marvellous because in the spirit of National Letter Writing Day (in the US at least), the Museum had decided to host some silly party for their largest (and thinnest) donors to unveil the first ever letter written to Father Christmas, or whatever the German for Father Christmas is, as it was apparently written there.

Normally I never ever bother with such small prizes. I'm more into sparkling, dazzling and millionaire treasures, but my client mentioned that the letter was worth a few million to him, so who was I to argue with such a refined (and foul) character?

And because this theft is technically for a wonderful holiday, I bought my small golden purse packed with a few wonderful surprises for anyone who tries to stop me.

Anyway I need a few quid these days for my sick mother, so I'm not exactly in a position to be too fussy with work. Then the rest of the money I'll probably keep some, donate some more to charity. I might even donate some to the museum.

Ha! Fat chance!

The sound of people shuffling caught my attention as I followed the crowds of (hot) young men and some other women towards the front of the room. Then I simply glided to the back of the crowd so I could watch everyone as we all stared at this posh elderly man who stood (way too) proudly on the stone steps.

I coughed a few times as I smelt all the horrible scents of aftershaves, perfumes and whatever unholy concoction these rich snobs covered their bodies in. I mean this is just ridiculous. A few sprays is fine fair enough, but an entire bottle! I don't want to choke to death on their smell!

As the elderly man starting to thank the donators, making a few awful jokes that only the snobbish manners of the rich would understand and introducing the letter. I started to notice a rather stunning man standing next to me.

He looked amazing in his custom-made tight black suit, his smooth handsome face and his stunning movie star smile. He seemed to be listening intently to the elderly man, but I didn't recognise him.

You see, I always make it a job before a job to memorise everyone's faces so I know exactly who will be there.

This hot guy wasn't meant to be here.

A drop of sweat rolled down my back. Now I had to play it cool, I couldn't act rash or question this guy because he would know what I was. And if he wasn't another thief then that would be a major cock-up on my part.

Believe me I may have done that before. Not a good idea.

The man leant closer to me. "You look beautiful tonight,"

If this man was simply a rich donator who wanted to unzip my dress then that would be okay, but there was something about this guy.

"Don't look so bad yourself," I said.

"What's your plan to get the letter? I was thinking about a simple fire alarm trick," the man said.

This guy might have been a thief, or he was lying which was my guess, but he couldn't have been a very good one given the letter was stored in a protected environment and extra security protocols were activated by the fire alarm.

"I don't know what you're talking about," I said, focusing on the speaker who looked like he was wrapping up.

"Who have you come as this time, Madame Francis?"

I felt my smile disappear as he said the name of one of my old aliases, he must have known of me for ages considering that one was from a job in France maybe... five years ago. At least I still had my escape routes if needed.

The stunning man stepped in front of me and

looked at my name badge, not that it would give him anything too useful.

"Elizabeth State, good name. She died ten years ago in the Caribbean you know,"

Now I ready wanted to leave, this guy knew way, way, way too much for being a simple rich man at a party. The man felt safe and good enough but there was something about him. He was hot as hell and yes, I would love him to unzip my dress tonight, but there was something off.

I went close to his ears, savouring the amazing smell of his aftershave.

"I presume you're a cop,"

The man almost laughed. "No, no Elizabeth. I not a cop. I see you haven't got my letter yet,"

I took a few steps back. This man couldn't have been my client, on the phone my client sounded older, richer and nowhere near as sexy.

The man kept smiling and changed his voice.

"In the package there will be an invitation and a dress. Go to the party, get the target and drop it off on the third seat of the Ten O'clock Tube at the nearest station,"

This wasn't right. They were the exact words of my client, but now this made no sense to me. I was well renowned as a master thief and yet my client felt the need to tail me to this event. They must have known I could get the letter-

The elderly man finished and started leading everyone up into the exhibition hall where the letter was.

I and this stunning but annoying as hell man followed.

"I wasn't expecting you here. But my fee is

doubled," I said.

The man frowned.

"I did tell you on my website. No tails. You must have read the terms and conditions?"

The man muttered something.

In truth I didn't have any terms, conditions or contracts on the site, but my clients always believed it. The amazing stupidity of the rich!

The crowd led me into a slightly smaller white room with the walls covered in breath-taking depictions of Christmas traditions through the centuries. From the pagans that started Christmas as we know it all the way to the wonderful (and far better) secular Christmases that we all know and love today, in all but name.

As the crowd of rich men and women slowly went around the room reading the stuff on the walls, my eyes were immediately drawn to the large glass cabinet in the middle of the room.

And inside it was a large, very long letter to Father Christmas in perfect condition and all written in German.

It was hard to believe that such a thing was worth so much money, but this hot as hell man clearly wanted it.

Then the idiot hot man decided to start walking straight over to the letter. Idiot!

I went over to him, wrapped my arm round his and guided him away.

"Oh honey, wait. We can look at the letter later, I want to read about Pagan festivals first," I said, shaking my head and smiling at my pretend lover.

The man smiled and went close to my ear. "What are you doing?"

"Oh honey, you've never done this before have you,"

"Never,"

If this was any other guy, I would easily make up some lame excuse to take him outside, then I would hit him, because this is my operation, my theft, my life and this idiot was going to muck it up.

Sadly this man was way too hot to hit and I wished I run my hands under that tight amazing suit and through his wonderfully thick hair, and his lips looked so soft, so warm, so-

The man started to guide me back over to the letter. This was getting out of hand.

"Listen," I said firmly. "No self-respecting thief goes for the prize straight away. That is how you get caught,"

The man stopped, kissed my head and pretended to talk about the pagan festivals.

"And I can see exactly what I need from here," I said.

"Like what?"

"There are five security guards. One in each corner and an undercover by the letter. The ones in the corners aren't a problem. The crowd is too thick and would delay them,"

"Who's the problem?" the man said, a little too enthusiastically for my taste.

"The one in the middle. He would get to us too quick,"

The man rubbed my arm as a few people looked at us. My fingers against my arm felt amazing, pure electricity flowed through me, I was enjoying him way too much.

"What about the glass cabinet itself? Looks

harmless," he asked.

Again if this was anyone else, I would have told them to break the cabinet, whilst I slipped into the crowd and let them get arrested. But sadly this stunning man was actually growing on me.

"Don't be stupid. The cabinet is electrified, it has a motion sensor and a heat sensor built into the case,"

The man frowned. "I thought you could break it,"

Now that was offensive!

"What do you take me for?" I asked.

"A hack,"

How I didn't slap him then I don't know.

A tall waitress was coming towards us with glasses of wonderfully golden champagne.

"Grab a glass," I said firmly.

We both grabbed one.

I couldn't help my smile but the next part was going to be great fun. Normally I did the whole acting chaos stuff with actual strangers but it might be even more fun acting with a person who I actually found attractive.

This was going to be fun.

"Are you a good actor?" I asked.

The man looked more concerned. "I suppose so. I did a few school plays. Lead role,"

Oh yes, this man was definitely rich. Only the rich snobs of the world ever compare school plays with proper acting and the level of acting needed for cons.

"Just play along. Go over and stand by the letter," I said.

We went over. Now the fun could begin!

I went over to him. "What are you doing! You

are so obsessed with this stupid letter!"

"Go away woman. Leave me alone for once in your miserable life. In fact. Get a life!"

"How dare you! I didn't even want to come to this shit hole museum tonight!" I shouted.

"Just go. Go back to our sorry ass kids. They're yours anyway. I don't want you, I don't want them. Now leave!"

The crowd muttered stuff.

"Maybe I will. Maybe I'll get a divorce!"

I went closer to the glass cabinet.

"Do whatever and take those bitching kids with you!"

The crowd didn't like that.

The security guards came over.

The man threw the champagne glass at me.

I ducked.

It splashed over the glass cabinet.

The security guards grabbed him. Taking him outside.

He smiled.

I pretended to cry and the elderly man in his tight suit from his speech on the steps came over and rubbed my back.

"Miss, I am so sorry you had to go through that,"

I hugged him. "And I'm so sorry for those horrible words I said. Your museum is lovely,"

I wiped a few tears away.

"Thank you. Now please stay and enjoy yourself. All five security guards will be downstairs making sure he stays away,"

As the elderly man left, I actually felt a little sad that that hot as hell stunning man wasn't going to be allowed back in. I was actually missing him!

But I did have a job to do, so onto stage two.

I went over to the glass cabinet and double checked if it was possible to see if any of the champagne had got inside.

It wasn't possible to tell. Good!

A rich young couple stood next to me so I whispered to them.

"I think the letter's damaged. I think there's champagne in there,"

The young woman looked horrified. She was clearly a history and art buff so she was perfect for this part. She rushed off to find the elderly man.

When she returned she was in a terrible (to her, wonderful to me) state and was begging the elderly man to open the glass cabinet to check on the *historical integrity* of the letter (Oh yes, she was one of those people).

The elderly man took out a key card from his suit pocket and swiped it over the glass cabinet. The cabinet hummed, vibrated and hissed as the pressurised air escaped. Making the air smell horribly of mustard.

Then the elderly man took off the glass and exposed the letter for all to see.

This was my chance.

I opened my gold purse, cracked a vial and waited.

The elderly man inspected the letter without picking it up.

The young woman and man were talking to the elderly man. He was distracted, my exit was clear.

I grabbed a small breath refresher from my purse filled with knock gas and I sprayed the three of them.

I grabbed the letter.

And run out.

I run down the stairs, past the security guards and out into the night.

***

A few hours later I stood on the cold lonely platform of the Tube Station with no one else there and only the cold concrete and white tiled walls to keep me company. Like every Tube Station after hours, the station smelt like urine, sick and spoiled food, but there was something refreshing about it tonight.

The foul smell kept me alert as I waited for the train and then I could easily escape into the chaos of London, change my identity and begin anew.

If it sounded like a lonely life, that was because it was in a way. It was partly why I did these jobs, thefts and other crazy things, because it meant I got to meet people and experience things that I never would be able to otherwise.

But tonight was surprisingly nice actually. I had never wanted to spend time with anyone before but that hot sexy man with his tight black suit, smooth handsome face and his amazing haircut. I really, really wanted him.

I wanted him to unzip my dress, run my fingers through his hair and down his suit to where my parcel could be delivered.

But I guess that was never going to happen, so again I would be alone doing random jobs over Christmas trying to raise more money for my sick mother, myself and the various charities that I'll donate to.

The sound of the Tube train in the distance made me step towards the edge of the platform as I waited for it to arrive when an arm wrapped round my waist.

I would recognise that amazing aftershave and those strong arms anywhere. That hot, sexy man had returned to me.

"You did well. My Letter?" the man asked.

I smiled and passed him the letter.

He ripped it up.

"What!" I shouted, as the pieces of the letter blew across the rails.

"Relax beautiful. The Letter's fake. I wrote it, aged it and donated it to the Museum. I only wanted to check if it was a good enough forgery,"

All I could do was stare at that amazing movie star smile as he probably felt really pleased with himself, and I couldn't blame him. Fooling the British Museum was no easy feat but he had to be here for something.

"You think I'm beautiful?" I asked.

As the train rolled into the station, the driver probably shocked that there were people here at all, that amazing hot sexy man kissed me on the lips. Hard. I savoured his soft lips and wondered what else was he hiding.

But at least I had my answer. He did find me beautiful, and I him.

I was half expecting him to say something but he gave me a smile. Not a malice, deceptive or evil smile that I would have expected for a forger and fellow criminal. But a smile that a schoolboy gives his prom date when he truly loves her.

He might have been a strange, hot, sexy criminal man who I barely knew, but as the train doors opened and we both went on, I looked forward to seeing where the train was going to lead us and hopefully our journey wouldn't end for a long, long time.

INTRODUCTION
Mood/ Genre: Fun Private Eye Mystery

As we move on to our penultimate Bettie English mystery of the Extravaganza, I wanted to take an extremely personal aspect of the holiday season and morph it into a great mystery story.

Since we all have some sort of social party, event or other thing going on in the holiday season. You might have a work's do, an office Christmas party or something special you do with your friends every year.

Personally, I always tend to go out with friends before Christmas as a little pre-Christmas celebration, in addition to the university Christmas socials that happen in early December, and those are great fun!

But my point is there are little social events that are unique to each group that make the holiday season extra special to each of us.

So how do Private Eyes celebrate such things?

Well that is the great focus of this short mystery

story, so please expect an enthralling fun story about everyone's favourite Private Eye as she prepares for one of the most important events in the Private Eye calendar.

And if you want to see Bettie and her team at the most important Private Eye event of the year, please check out the gripping, unputdownable book *The Federation Protects* available at all major booksellers from August 2023.

Enjoy!

PRIVATE EYE, CONVENTION AND CHRISTMAS

"What's EyeFoodCon aunty?"

When Bettie heard her nephew Sean ask her that simple question, she wasn't really sure how to answer it. As a private eye she had just known what it was for as long as she could remember.

Bettie looked at her tall slim nephew and tried to think about how to answer such a strange question, that she knew what it was, she just didn't know how to explain it to someone who wasn't a private eye.

The sounds of people talking, chatting and laughing on the awfully cold December night made Bettie shiver. She hated the cold so she pulled her long black overcoat tighter and ignored her nephew.

As much as Bettie loved him, she wanted, needed to buy herself a few extra seconds so she could think of an answer to his question.

Bettie watched the little families walk around with the occasional parent moaning at their overexcited kids and other people were weighed down with their Christmas shopping in Bluewater shopping centre in southeast England.

She was glad her and Sean hadn't bought that much stuff tonight but she did need to press on with their shopping. That was probably the only downside to the Christmas season, even more so as a private eye, there were so many cases at Christmas time that it made Christmas shopping in advance impossible.

Bettie bit her lip as she wondered how many more presents she needed to buy. There was her sister, her boyfriend and more.

As she pushed those panicked thoughts away, Bettie watched the busy crowd around them go in and out of shops like their lives depended on it, it seemed them too needed to get lots of presents before the big day.

The smell of rich Christmas spices filled the air as Bettie and Sean kept walking on, gliding through the crowd and walking like they were on a mission. Because in a way they were, Bettie had to get all the presents tonight considering the all the private eye parties started soon.

With the smell of the Christmas spices getting stronger with hints of sweat that made her mouth taste of Christmas cake, Bettie kept gliding through the crowd as her eyes narrowed for the next shop she needed.

"What's EyeFoodCon aunty?" Sean asked again walking next to her.

Bettie smiled. "It's hard to explain Sean. It's a little private holiday for private eyes,"

"Is it like a Christmas party?"

Bettie stepped out of the way of a big family of shoppers and saw a massive wonderful sign in the distance of a perfume shop she needed to go to for her sister. She had no idea why her sister wanted some expensive perfume that she was never going to wear, but Bettie just wanted to keep the peace, love her sister and get on with the rest of the shopping.

The only problem was the sea of busy (grumpy) shoppers in her way.

"Aunty?" Sean asked.

Bettie took Sean's hand like she did when he was a toddler and guided him through the sea of people.

"In a way yes," Bettie said. "It was started a few years back by the Jewish and Muslim private eyes,"

Bettie gently knocked a shopper out of the way so her and Sean could continue through the crowd.

"They heard all their private eye friends were busy and missing over Christmas as they were celebrating with the family. So the Professional Private Investigator Society created EyeFoodCon as a secular celebration for everyone,"

"Ah," Sean said.

After making it through the massive sea of grumpy, busy shoppers, Bettie loved the amazing smell of the sweet flowery perfume in the massive shop she entered.

Bettie cocked her head for a moment as she

didn't remember the shop being this big before, but she loved the long white walls of colour perfume bottles in all their different shapes, sizes and prices.

She wanted to shake her head when she saw Sean walk over to the unisex (but more feminine) perfume as she knew for a fact that he was getting it for himself.

The smell of the sweet flowery perfume kept getting stronger but Bettie knew something was off. It was too strong for someone just spraying.

Bettie stared at the horribly shiny white floor and her eyes widened when she saw a smashed bottle of perfume a few metres from her.

She walked over and had to cover her nose with her hand, Bettie normally loved that perfume but it was way too strong when she was breathing in a whole bottle of it.

"You're going to have to pay for that Miss," a woman said.

Bettie looked at the tall business-like woman who had said that, and she shook her head. It was silly that this woman thought Bettie had done it, she had only just got here.

"I found it like this," Bettie said.

The woman shook her head. "They all say that. Come with me and you can pay for it at the tills,"

"I didn't break it. I'm innocent. Check your cameras,"

The woman frowned. "I know what I saw,"

Bettie couldn't believe how silly this woman was,

she supposed the woman could be fed up with all the stealing and breaking that normally happens at Christmas, but Bettie wasn't guilty.

"Aunty?" Sean said walking over.

"Sean how are you?" the woman asked. "How's Harry? We have a new stock that aftershave he likes,"

Bettie wanted to shake her head so badly, trust Sean to walk into a scene and instantly know how to calm it down. That was probably why she had bought him just in case.

"Thank you, I'll take a bottle. What were you talking to my aunty about?"

Bettie couldn't believe it when the woman looked at her and explained everything to Sean like Bettie was the worse criminal ever.

Sean nodded. "I know my Aunty seems shifty, criminal and a bit crazy but she's safe,"

How Bettie didn't playfully hit him she didn't know.

"I can assure you my Aunty didn't break anything. She's honest and she could help you,"

Bettie felt like she was going to regret this for sure, maybe she should have bought her boyfriend Graham like he had suggested.

Bettie stepped forward. "Help you how,"

"Your nephew mentions you're a Private Investigator,"

As much as Bettie wanted to correct her as she loved the more playful term Private Eye, Bettie knew this probably wasn't the time considering whoever this woman was still thought she was guilty.

"Bettie English Private Eye at your service,"

The woman nodded. "Our cameras aren't working at the moment and… my boss isn't happy with me. If I hire you to watch the store for a couple of hours-"

Bettie's mouth dropped. "Wait! I have Christmas shopping to do. I have a mini-convention to buy food for and… it's Christmas soon,"

"Aunty I can do the shopping for you,"

Bettie wanted to protest but she supposed she loved Sean too much and he was being nice, but Bettie didn't want to do this.

"How much?" Bettie asked.

"We paid the last security person a hundred pounds for the night,"

Bettie didn't know whether to be shocked, pleased or horrified that a security person is actually given that much money for a few hours of work. But the sound of a hundred pounds for two little hours, it did sound good.

It was technically her turn to host and pay for most of EyeFoodCon so that money would easily pay for it.

"Hundred pounds for the night. Extra twenty for false accusations," Bettie said.

The woman frowned.

"And throw it two bottles of whatever Sean wants since you hesitated," Bettie said smiling.

"Fine. I trust you know how to look innocent

and like a random shopper,"

As she watched the woman and Sean walk off so he could choose what he wanted, Bettie looked around the massive store and rolled her eyes. Some days it really sucked to be a private eye but a hundred pounds was a hundred pounds that she didn't have before, and maybe she could find a nice present for Graham to buy her.

The advantages of borrowing his credit card earlier!

Walking up the rows of perfume bottles, Bettie didn't know how these two hours were going to go, surely a perfume shop didn't see that much crime at Christmas.

***

After an hour and forty-five minutes, Bettie couldn't believe how brilliant this actually was, at first she thought she was going to hate it with a passion, but she didn't.

Bettie had already found some great new perfumes that she loved, she found the foul smelling one that her dad loved and she even found a new special one for herself that she might wear on Christmas day.

But Bettie still didn't want to buy any of them because as much as they were great perfumes, they weren't cheap and a hundred pounds was not going to cover it. Not by a long shot.

Bettie ran her fingers over the cold white shelves as she looked at all the perfume and aftershave bottles in all their different sizes, shapes and colours. The bottles were beautiful but Bettie remembered from her business study classes at school that was all part of the visual appeal. It did nothing practical, except from increase the prices.

The sound of customers talking, trying on perfume and judging the smells echoed all around the massive shop as Bettie waited for her two hours to be up.

Yet Bettie could have sworn there was another sound she was hearing, it was like the low quiet voices of two people conspiring to do something.

Bettie had hated the idea of people stealing from the start, it was Christmas for crying out loud, this was not a time for stealing, it was a time for love, giving and caring.

Walking to the end of the shelf she was looking at, Bettie's eyes narrowed on the two young women that were close together and trying on different perfumes.

To other people they may not have looked like criminals or would-be shoplifters, but Bettie recognised the closeness, quiet voices and the long expensive coats of the two girls.

It reminded Bettie of her own troublesome streak when she was a teenager, if that was the case with these two women then Bettie supposed she could get rid of them without any major problems.

But these women weren't teenagers, they were fully-fledged adults who were looking like they were going to try and steal something.

After a few moments of watching, Bettie noticed that one of the women had got out her phone and was pretending to take a phone call. Bettie shook her head as she watched the perfectly clear black screen of the girl's phone, if you're going to pretend to take a pretend phone call you need to make it a bit more convincing.

Bettie wondered if she should get the woman or the manager to deal with them, but she wasn't going to risk losing her hundred pounds for simply *failing* to do her assigned job. She wasn't risking any comments like that.

As the woman with the phone pretended to nod, promise the person on the other side of the call she'd take a picture and check the surroundings (completely missing Bettie). Bettie knew that this woman was an amateur, there was no way these two had done shoplifting before.

If Bettie was doing this she would have been in the car park driving home by now.

Then Bettie watched in horror as the two women did a final check of the store, missed Bettie and just picked up the perfumes like it was nothing and placed it in their coat pockets.

Bettie walked towards them. The two women pretended to act normal.

"I know what you just did," Bettie said.

"We ain't steal nothing," the pretend phone caller said.

Bettie shook her head. "I finish my 'shift' in two minutes. I do not want to be here any longer than I have to be. Just apologise, pay for the perfumes and go,"

"We ain't steal nothing," they both said together.

Bettie hated this entire thing, she had Christmas shopping to do, EyeFoodCon to plan and buy for and on top of all of that she no longer wanted to be in some perfume shop.

"Empty your pockets," Bettie said firmly.

The two women ran.

Bettie ran after them.

Her feet pounded the floor.

The two women were fast.

Bettie couldn't let them leave the shop.

She looked around.

The women were close to the exit.

There were a sea of shoppers.

Bettie was going to lose them.

Bettie panicked.

Picked up a perfume bottle.

Threw it.

It smashed on the woman's back.

She fell forward.

Catching the other woman.

There was something oddly satisfying around that Bettie realised as she walked over and stood over the two injured women were who frowning and probably wished they had tried another shop.

The tall business-like woman ran over to Bettie.

"Miss English! What have you done?"

"These two women were stealing. I stopped them. You own me my hundred pounds,"

"You damaged my store! You broke a bottle of perfume! You…"

Bettie shook her head. "My hundred pounds and extra twenty please. Or I will call your head office and tell them you hired a private eye on company time and money without approval,"

Bettie couldn't help but smile as the woman looked so shocked and panicked as if this was the first time ever she had been challenged.

"Fine Miss English," the woman said giving Bettie her money.

"Let's do this again some time," Bettie said leaving the shop.

"Let's not," Bettie heard the woman muttered.

The moment she left the shop, Bettie glided into the sea of busy grumpy shoppers and called Sean. As the phone dialled she was slightly surprised how good she was feeling after all of that, it felt great to be out in December, doing her shopping and stopping crime at the same time.

But now she had to get on with the most important event in the Private Eye calendar, EyeFoodCon.

Sean picked up his phone.

Bettie smiled. "Hi Sean, want to come to EyeFoodCon with me?"

***

A few days later Bettie sat on a terribly cold chair on the head of a long, long oak table with wonderfully decorated Christmas decorations covering the entire walls.

Bettie loved all their baubles, tinsel and the wreaths that covered the walls of the business room that she had hired especially for the convention.

And as she watched all the different Private Eyes in all their different ethnicities, sizes and heights eat the beautiful golden, crispy food in front of them, and the rest of the juicy meats and other sweet treats that covered the entire length of the table, Bettie realised something precious.

The sound of happy Private Eyes talking, chatting and laughing with one another reminded Bettie how EyeFoodCon should be explained to anyone.

Bettie looked at Sean who was laughing with a young woman at the table and he saw her.

Bettie leaned closer to Sean. "You see all this,"

Sean looked around and nodded.

"This is what EyeFoodCon is all about. No matter your race, religion, preferences, whatever. You are always welcome in the Private Eye community. We are all a family,"

Sean smiled at that.

"So what is EyeFoodCon you ask," Bettie said.

Sean leant closer.

"EyeFoodCon is about community and the secular side of Christmas. I love all Private Eyes no matter who they are and I welcome them all. This mini-convention is a reminder of that at this time of year,"

Sean looked around a final time.

"Just because we don't all celebrate Christmas doesn't mean we can't love, give and support each other at this time of year,"

Just saying that made Bettie feel all Christmassy and merry because she knew that was all the truth, and that's why she loved being a Private Eye because it truly was a community.

A loving, supporting and amazing community for all.

Bettie was a bit surprised when Sean kissed her cheek and held her hands.

"Merry Christmas Aunty,"

Bettie stood up and said to everyone: "A Merry Christmas, New Year and all the other celebrations to everyone,"

INTRODUCTION

Mood/ Genre: Light Contemporary Fantasy

For the next story in the holiday Extravaganza, I really wanted to explore a very fundamental question about the holiday season, love and death.

If you could talk to a loved one again, would you do it?

Now I fully appreciate that this might not sound like a very light topic for the holiday season, but given how the holidays are meant to be about love, family and friends. I don't really think there is a better topic for this time of year.

So in this next Extravaganza story, please expect a grieving man, some souls and most importantly some magic.

Enjoy!

SOULCASTER

Snow crunched under my feet as I walked through the beautiful snowy forest, I loved the way the snow blanketed the massive tall pine trees like it was some winter wonderland. This was the first time in years I had felt… good, maybe even good since my wife died, and yet I was here to do something silly.

Up ahead I saw a bright flickering fire with tall shadows of people walking around it, I looked forward to the amazing warmth of those tall flames, anything was better than the bitter cold that was trying to bite at me.

Now I was never a religious person, I hated religion with a passion, but I supposed I had grown so sad, miserable and depressed over the years since my dear sweet wife died, I had grown too desperate.

The smell of cold smoke filled the air wonderfully as it reminded me of my delicious favourite barbecues as a child. I got close to the roaring fire and I started to hear little whispers from the people round the fire.

I knew I had probably gone crazy when I had checked out the online advert for the so-called Soulcaster that could apparently make my life better and allow me to speak to my dead wife one final time.

Absolutely rubbish.

But I saw the online advert a few more times and I guess I got worn down so I clicked on it, checked out the details and decided to come here.

All I knew for sure was this Soulcaster woman (or man) was meant to be some kind of ancient person who had direct ties to the Pagans. Well, given it's the freezing dead of winter in the southeast of England, I suppose it had to be pagans or whatever.

Not that I know anything about the pagans.

I got closer to the fire and I couldn't understand it but it looked as if the entire fire had changed since I last focused on it.

Now the fire looked larger with tens of tall, short and medium sized people around it holding out their hands to get warm. I couldn't blame them. It was freezing out here, apparently the canopy in the forest was meant to give it some warmth but that clearly wasn't happening.

I heard the whispers clearer now and even then I didn't understand. Normally I could understand everyone, no matter how bad their English, but these whispers, these people weren't speaking English. It sounded Latin or something.

Something in the back of my mind wanted me to

turn around and never ever return here, but there was a part of me that wanted to continue. It was probably the part of me that decades working as a scientist had developed and matured.

I had to know what was going on here.

I walked straight up to the fire and looked at its roaring, swirling and whirling flames that dramatically rose and fall in defiance of the natural wind that was blowing. But what made me even more curious was how the person in all their different sizes, heights and ethnicities weren't looking or taking any notice of me.

That was strange.

I looked around and wondered what they were doing, there was no one else around me but still all these people were staring at the fire and whispering in Latin to each other.

Now something inside me was telling me to leave but then I started to hear something like a whooshing sound behind me.

I looked around and saw a massive Christmas tree appear with thousands of lights, baubles and golden tinsel hanging off the tree perfectly. I couldn't believe my eyes, the tree was so beautiful, perfect and filled the air with the joyous hum of Christmas Spirit.

Walking over to it, my eyes narrowed and I was determined to figure out what this was. I had to channel my inner scientist because there had to be a logical explanation to this, the tree wasn't there a moment ago, and out of all the strange things I had seen in my life this had to top the list.

"Do you know what Soul Day is?" an old lady said to me.

I blinked and jumped.

A little old Lady was hunched over in front of me wearing an ugly long dark cloak with massive holes. I wanted to offer her my own coat or offer her something to help her, I didn't want to see an old lady cold on this night.

But the more I looked at this old lady, the older she appeared to be.

She raised her head slightly and my eyes widened when I saw how dead, glassy and lifeless her own eyes were. It was almost like her eyes were dead and yet she endured.

Now I mention it, her face looked pretty dead too. Her skin was dry, broken and cracked.

As much as I wanted to offer my help (I always want to help people), I got the sense from her that it was safer not to get too close to her.

Then I remembered the question.

"Soul Day?" I asked.

"Yes young man," she said.

I wanted to laugh at that, I wasn't young, I was ancient according to my grandchildren and all the neighbour kids.

"Soul Day is the day better than Christmas," she said.

I doubted it, for me Christmas was the only day I felt alive, happy and like life was worth living. I got to see my children, my grandchildren and spend quality time with them. To me that was the most precious thing ever.

"Soul Day is when all the souls of the dead come to us once more and we can listen," she said smiling at me.

I wanted to ask her so many questions, about my wife, my family, my future, but I didn't push her. Whoever she was I got the feeling it was better not to push her, and instead just let her do the talking.

"You come here because someone wills it. I can see something in you. A shadow. A Loom. No, sorry, a looming death. A wave of sadness that claims your family and destroys all their Christmases to come,"

My mouth dropped. I didn't want that for my family, I wanted them to enjoy life, be happy and merry. They didn't deserve to be sad.

The woman extended a long pointy finger and pointed at my head.

"You're going to die,"

That was impossible for this random stranger to know, I hadn't told anyone presides my own family and they wouldn't tell anyone. I had only found out about the brain tumour a few weeks ago and the doctors said it might still be treatable so they needed to do some more tests.

"Whoever wills you to come here is here. They walk through the forest. The cold snow biting at their feet. They come here to speak to you,"

I wasn't having any of this nonsense coming from the woman. It was impossible for her to know anything, she couldn't have known about my tumour, she couldn't have known anyone was coming and she couldn't have known anything about me.

I didn't even know her.

"Leave me alone," I said walking towards the fire.

But I stopped as soon as I saw the fire had changed yet again with the flames still roaring but the flames were smaller, blue and colder.

"What is this place?" I asked.

I felt the old lady's body warmth against my back but I didn't feel her press into me.

"Look at the people," she said.

As I looked at them I didn't see anything special about them. There were so many people in all their different sizes, heights and clothing that there wasn't anything too interesting to see. Except one thing.

They weren't speaking Latin anymore.

Instead they were just standing there staring straight at me like I was the only thing in the world at that point.

"Why are they staring at me?" I asked.

"They see something in you. They see the same as me. We all see a looming death,"

"What is all this? What is Soul Day?" I said firmly.

The old lady laughed. "Soul Day is what you make it. It is meant to protect your Soul. It is meant to kill it. It is meant to save it,"

I threw up my arms in disbelief. Whatever this

weird online advert was meant to be, it was clearly meant to be some sort of prank, lie or whatever.

I didn't care anymore.

I was going home.

"Hubby?" a young woman said behind me.

As I looked at the woman my eyes widened as I stare the ghostly form of my late wife, her skin youthful, her hair long and golden and her clothes exactly like the night I met her in the 60s.

Her face looked so beautiful, calm and stunning but I didn't want to believe this was my wife. My wife, my stunning wife was dead, this couldn't be her. There was always a logical explanation and her being alive was not one of them!

"You see the shadow. The Loom. The Looming Death over him," the old lady said to my wife.

My wife frowned. "I do. Hubby, what is wrong?"

I saw the old lady walk away. "You aren't real. My wife is dead. I don't care what your acting school is paying you, don't pretend to be the dead!"

"You always were a scientific one. You never did believe in anything else. I am here hubby,"

As much as I wanted to believe it was her, I couldn't. There were no such things as ghosts, monsters or the supernatural. My wife couldn't be in front of me unless she was a pile of ash.

"I'm leaving. Good luck with your acting classes. You're good, I'll give you that,"

I was about to walk far, far away from this strange, god forsaken place when the old lady appeared holding out a large golden Bauble.

I'll admit it was beautiful with the stunning reflection of the dancing flames but again that wasn't possible. The flames were so small.

Then I looked at the fire.

All the people were gone and the fire was a raging inferno. The sound of the flames was deafening and now I sank to my knees in confusion.

"Please. What is happening here?" I asked my voice full of emotion.

My wife knelt next to me. "I wanted you here tonight. In the Place-After-Earth, I got to see what became of my family,"

I looked at her, my eyes watery.

"Hubby. You die soon. Our family falls apart. Some hate you for being so grumpy, sad and depressed. Some defend you. All fall to pieces. All turn to ash. Our Family ends,"

That wasn't true. I was a great person and everyone understood that my wife had died and I was finding life hard. They wouldn't hate me. They…

My wife held my hand. I almost jumped at the coldness.

"Hubby. When you come here and are reunited with me. What do you want to watch from above? Your family fall apart or your family love each other, celebrate and respect you,"

I didn't know what to say. I still couldn't believe this was my wife, my stunning wife that I had loved for decades and mourned for so long recently.

But there was something in her voice that made it all sound so truthful.

My wife disappeared to be replaced with a large ball of golden swirling light. The light rushed past me. I saw it go into the golden bauble the old lady was holding.

"Bring her back!" I shouted.

The Old Lady laughed and gestured me to stand up.

"You still want to know what Soul Day is truly about?"

I nodded.

"The Shadow grows within your head. The Looming Death grows ever closer. The Tsunami of Sadness grows stronger every second ready to consume all those you loved,"

"Please. What must I do?" I asked.

"Soul Day is the one time of the year where I come out from the past and into the future. The veils between the past, present, future and the living and the dead are so weak. Not even paper thin. So I picked this year to come and I willed thirteen people to come. And you are the last,"

I felt my stomach tighten.

"What happened to the other twelve?"

The Old Lady shook her head. "They forsaken me. They choose to spend Soul Day by spending their souls and damning their world to grief, terror and misery,"

"I won't," I said more out of instinct than

thought but I still smiled.

The Old Lady nodded. "Then change. You have exactly three months to live. I will come knocking in the dead of the night. So you love, respect and adore your family or your soul will be damned,"

I couldn't do anything but nod and smile to that. It sounded crazy, stupid and silly but it also sounded so right, like it was the truth and nothing else was going to convince me otherwise.

I knew I had to go home call my family, invite them round for dinner tomorrow and make sure tomorrow was the start of a wonderful final three months.

"Thank you," I said to her. "I'll make sure my family hear the story of Soul Day and why it is the most important Day of the year,"

The Old Lady smiled and slowly started to disappear.

"Then go but never forget the Shadow. The Looming Death. Nor the Tidal Wave of Sadness. It will come but only you can stop it. So love, respect, adore your family til we meet again,"

As I left the strange fire, forest and the Soulcaster, I was going to be the greatest father, grandfather and person in the world to make sure my family were going to be strong after I died.

But about the whole Soul Day thing, I actually think it could be the start of something great and an amazing legacy for me and my family. Because at the end of the day, my family are my love, my life and my future.

MADE-UP HOLIDAYS COLLECTION

INTRODUCTION
Mood/ Genre: Heart-warming Contemporary Fantasy

To continue with the fantasy section of this Extravaganza, we turn our attention to a certain aspect of Christmas and the holiday season that the vast majority of us thankfully never ever have had to experience.

And that is rejection.

Now please relax, the story itself is extremely heart-warming that is why I wrote the story, because I wanted to remind us all that Christmas is a magic time of year and amazing things can happen.

So this is why I choose this story to be the one that goes out on Christmas Eve, because there will sadly be people on Earth tonight that aren't spending time with loved ones, family and their friends.

Some people will be kicked out on the streets, abandoned and unloved by their families because of what they are, who they love and many more factors.

But if anything else, this story truly reminds us of the need, desire and utter magic that family provides us with. Not necessarily a blood family, but another much more precious kind.

So please expect a wonderfully heart-warming fantasy story about love, magic and what the true meaning of Christmas is all about.

Enjoy!

ALL FEAST

Ryan walked down the little path through the massive forest beside his amazing, wonderful boyfriend Tao, and he wouldn't have it any other way. The trees were massive thick pines filling the air with their sweet piney scents that Ryan really liked.

He wasn't sure why Tao was leading him through the forest on a path that was clearly never used on Christmas Eve. In his ideal world Ryan would have loved Tao to invite him round, spend the evening with him and hopefully roll around in a bed together.

But there was something about Tao that made Ryan sure he wasn't interested in taking their relationship to the next level yet. Ryan wished he would, but he was patient and he did love Tao, so he would wait.

The sound of birds, elves and phoenixes echoed around the forest as the sun started to set. Ryan liked the bitter coldness of winter, there was something pleasant about its bite. And if anything else, it might provide the perfect excuse for him to snuggle up next to Tao, wherever he was leading him.

From everything he had heard about the forest, Ryan really didn't know anything of interest up here, the forest was largely endless miles of trees and lakes and a few cabins sprinkled in from a bygone age, when humans thought it was right to hunt down the magical creatures that lived in these parts.

Ryan looked up at Tao as he continued to lead them on. Tao wore his normal tight blue jeans that left nothing to the imagination, his black hiking boots and a great black hoody.

And there was just something about Tao, maybe it was the way he walked, smiled and just projected confidence that Ryan loved so much about him.

When Ryan saw Tao look back at him and smile, he couldn't believe how great he felt. He was outside with the man he loved, going to a secret place for Christmas, hopefully. For Christmas Eve might have been about family traditionally but as his family had so plainly put it to him a few months ago, there was nothing traditional, right or sane about what Ryan loved.

They didn't care too much about family then. And Ryan didn't care too much either.

The smell of smoke made Ryan look up and he stopped when he saw a large stone mansion in the middle of a clearing. Ryan had heard of rich old people building great mansions in these parts of the woods decades ago, but he had always believed them to be just myths and legends.

But this mansion was stunning, Ryan hoped that this was where Tao was going to take him, the warm, ancient setting would be so romantic, so perfect and just what Ryan needed after a bad year.

Tao turned around. Ryan loved his smooth cheeks, stunning longish hair and that amazing smile that could melt even the toughest of hearts.

"Happy All Feast Beautiful," Tao said walking towards the mansion.

Ryan just stood there. The All Feast? He had never heard of such a thing, Tao had never mentioned it, Ryan didn't celebrate or know of it. What had he just walked into? Or perhaps the better question was, what had his boyfriend led him into?

After he walked through the front door, Ryan was stunned by the ancient wooden hallway and beautiful stone staircase that went up steeply and the canvas painting on the walls were impressive. This definitely was once home to a rich, spoiled person. No normal person could afford such things, at least not to as grand a scale.

The sound of two distinctive sets of footsteps that came out of the kitchen area at the end of the hallway, and Ryan was pleasantly surprised to see another two young, loved up men. Two friends of Tao.

Ryan had met Jim with his bright ginger hair and Francis a number of times over the past few months, from what he could tell they were Tao's best friends and they had been together since last Christmas when Jim's family had thrown him on the streets. Ryan wasn't sure why, it was either because he was gay or they were too poor to feed him, and him being gay was the perfect excuse to get rid of him.

But Ryan was a little surprised that he was really glad to see them. He liked them, they were both great people, and as sad as it sounded, any friend of Tao was a friend of his. Yet his entire body relaxed at the sight of them.

It was probably because Ryan had just wanted to be round people who respected his choices and weren't going to give him so much grief.

"Hi," Ryan said to both of them.

Jim and Francis both smiled at him. It wasn't a normal smile by any means, there was definitely something going on, Ryan just wanted to find out what.

"Tao, have you told him? Have you told him?" Jim said, his voice high pitched and excited.

Tao's fingers grazed Ryan's shoulder, Ryan savoured the feeling.

"Na, I thought we tell him later," Tao said, giving Jim and Francis a friendly hug.

Ryan had no idea what All Feast was, it was clearly something important to the three of them. Why didn't they just tell him? Ryan wanted, needed to know.

He almost started to feel left out, like back in school when the cool kids knew something great and the wannabes didn't.

"Beautiful?" Tao said.

Ryan quickly smiled and hoped Tao didn't think he was jealous or too desperate to learn the secret.

Jim walked back into the kitchen.

"So what's All Feast?" Ryan asked.

Francis smiled. "Ya'll find out soon enough,"

Jim came back holding a sort of sweatshirt. "Here, Put it on please,"

Jim threw the sweatshirt over to Ryan.

It was only then that Ryan looked at Jim and Francis and noticed that they were both wearing the exact same black sweatshirt with a Christmas pudding in the middle. Surely it was a couple thing.

But Tao gently rubbed Ryan's shoulder. "Please,"

Ryan always loved how velvety and beautiful Tao's voice was, so he could hardly refuse.

"Come on Laddie, ya can change upstairs if ya shy. I can explain something to ya too," Francis said, walking up the stone staircase.

Ryan followed.

As they walked into a wonderfully large bedroom with brown oak walls and a massive old bed into the middle fit for a king (or two in this case), Ryan felt the excitement build within him. He would love to spend the night (or forever) in a place like this. It would be amazing to pretend to be a king and actually have some power after the year he had had.

Ryan took off his shirt and started to put on the sweatshirt.

"So what is All Feast?" Ryan said, his voice a little more desperate than he wanted.

Francis laughed. "I did tell Tao to tell ya before ya came. It is great to have ya though. Jim's been wanting to have ya for months,"

"Have me for what?"

"For All Feast. Our version of Christmas,"

Ryan finished putting on the sweatshirt, realising it was a little tight and left nothing to the imagination, but at least Tao would see his slight muscles.

"Sorry. Wrong size. I'll remember for next year,"

Ryan was surprised at that. No one had ever fussed over him like that before, Ryan's entire life had been a case of if you don't like it, tough, be grateful you little so and so. Ryan bit back a small swell of emotion, he didn't want to feel so emotional but that simple sentence had meant so much to him.

"Ya know how Christmas is all about family, food and love?" Francis said.

Ryan nodded.

"Ma Family is good. Support, respect, love me. Don't really care if I'm there or not. Jim's fam, well, kicked him out and poor to the limit. Tossed him out the second they could,"

Ryan nodded and gestured Francis to stop. He really didn't want to hear what happened to Tao, he already knew. He hated Tao's family for what they did to him, all the hate, abuse and outrage aimed at him every hour of every day.

At least Ryan never had to meet them with Tao

cutting them out of his life.

"Yea, sorry I forgot ya two talk about it," Francis said. "And yours? Tao told us some,"

Ryan smiled. "My family. There's arguing, hate and no respect for my choices. I'm wrong, unnatural and deserve to have the gay beaten out of me with a big stick,"

Francis laughed hard at that. "The things peeps believe,"

Ryan smiled, truly smiled. Realising it was the first time he had smiled in a long, long time with anyone else but Tao. It felt good, it felt great, it felt right.

"All Feast?" Ryan asked.

"Oh yea, none of us have love, food and family. So made our own, there's no religion, no hate, no nothing. The three of us have to agree on everything, no one can come unless we want to and everything is done together,"

Ryan took a step back. That all sounded strangely wonderful, a Christmas or Christmas time without any arguing about the decorations, lights or anything else. Christmas could be what it was meant to be about, loving your family.

Family didn't have to be blood and that was what Ryan loved about gays, because it was like one big family. Especially with his wonderful, beautiful Tao and his two friends.

Ryan just felt at home here, there was something so peaceful, comfortable and even magical about the entire thing. At last after a rough start to his life and everything that happened a few months ago, he could finally start to live life how he wanted and loved who he wanted without any negatives.

It felt like a massive weight had just lifted and Ryan couldn't wait to celebrate All Feast with his new forged family.

"So ya know All Feast is what it meant to be. A Feast for All no matter who or what ya are, ya are always welcome here. And Tao begged me to let ya come. I was always going to say yes, but it was funny seeing him beg,"

Ryan felt another wave of emotion flood him, he had never known Tao to show that much emotion about him. Ryan wasn't sure if Tao was even really into him anymore, he hadn't been as emotional, passionate or loving towards him lately.

But maybe Ryan was wrong. He hoped so, so badly.

"Come on Laddie, gonna make more foods for the Feast. Tao didn't tell me what ya wanted for the Feast, so…"

It was silly that Ryan was so shocked, but to him, he had never been asked these questions. No one had ever cared about him this much before. He had always been given things and forced to enjoy them, it never mattered what he wanted.

But it did here.

"Biscuits?" Ryan forced out.

Francis cocked his head. "Biscuits? I… oh Jim

likes them too. Ginger nut okay,"

Gays, nuts and... Ryan really tried hard not to make a joke. But everyone was family here, so Ryan knew he had to start relaxing and unlearning all the things he had taught himself over the years. Because he had to act straight, he had to be a certain way.

But now... now he could be himself.

Yet the joke moment had definitely passed now anyway.

"Yea ginger nuts are great," Ryan said.

Francis smiled. "You're telling me,"

After they went back downstairs and into the kitchen, Francis gestured to Jim to come with him and Ryan went into the kitchen.

The house might have been old but the kitchen was stunning. Ryan had always had a soft spot for "real" kitchens with a massive kitchen island in the middle with a large oven, plenty of brown cupboards and most importantly Tao standing at the island mixing a bowl.

Ryan went up behind him, wrapped his arms around Tao and rested his head on Tao's strong shoulders.

"Thank you for this," Ryan said, kissing Tao's neck. "Who's house is this?"

Ryan saw Tao smile. "Ya welcome. It's mine now. My fam signed it over to me as a peace offering months ago. It didn't work but I, we, have a house,"

Ryan ignored the *we* part, that would get him way too emotional. That was for sure.

"What you making?" Ryan asked.

"You always said you liked ginger nuts at Christmas,"

Ryan couldn't speak as he just let his stomach tense and relax. Tao was amazing that was for sure.

"No one has ever done this for me before. Why you doing it?" Ryan asked.

Tao spun around and wrapped his own arms around Ryan.

"Because you're important to me. I want you to become part of my life and my family,"

Ryan felt his eyes wet at the sound of someone actually wanting him.

"Live with me. Be with me. Love with me," Tao said, grazing Ryan's lips.

"Done," Ryan said, kissing him.

And as Tao sadly broke the kiss and turned back to mixing up the mixture in the bowl, Ryan just stood there for a moment, savouring the feel of Tao against him.

This really was going to be the start of an amazing new life with people who actually loved with and wanted him around. That feeling would definitely take time to get used to but Ryan didn't mind in the slightest.

Ryan ran his hands up Tao before he broke away and grabbed a mixing bowl of his own, and stared at the stunning man who he was hopefully, happily going to spend the rest of his life with.

It didn't matter what happened in his life now,

Ryan had his family, an amazing boyfriend and soon a wonderful All Feast that was going to be the first of many more to come.

INTRODUCTION

Mood/ Genre: Light Private Eye Mystery

After Christmas and the big feast, there can occasionally (always) be tons of food leftover, leaving some with a few different options depending on the family. You could wrap up the food and eat it over the next few days, you could bin it (please don't do that) or you could reuse it in some creative way.

Personally, me and my family tend to save the leftovers after Christmas day dinner and pick at it for the rest of Christmas Day before dessert.

Then as there is always plenty of food leftover including desserts, we save it and reuse it on my mum's birthday which is a few days after Christmas and then we try and use it all up before it goes off.

So when I was asked to submit a short story to a Christmas anthology based on a Made-Up Holiday, I knew that I had to create a holiday based on all this leftover food.

Of course, I won't spoil the story in the slightest, but as you read our final (and probably best) Bettie English short story of the Holiday Extravaganza. I can promise you, you're in for a very interesting, enthralling mystery centred around leftover food.

And if you want to read more about the Bettie English's mysteries, then you will love the first full-length book in the series *A Very Private Woman* available from all major booksellers in electronic and paper from March 2023.

Enjoy!

GREAT GIVE AWAY

Bettie English, Private Eye, loved her mother's birthday. It was always an amazing day filled with laughter, love and plenty of tasty food. But as she stood on the pavement of a long road with little houses lining each side of it, she was hardly impressed.

She had told her boyfriend, who was currently bent over the engine of her red car, to take a right then a left. That wasn't hard. It was easy, she had done it hundreds of times and her sister had done it drunk even more times.

But no. Her boyfriend Detective Graham had to take left then right, leading them to this God forsaken little road (Street?) with pretty little houses far away from her mother's house and then the car broken down.

Bettie was not impressed!

She didn't even know if Graham knew anything about cars. He was a detective, he was amazing at his job, but as she had learnt way too many times recently if she told him to put his mind to anything else, he was sexy and hot as hell, but next to useless.

Bettie had to admit watching Graham in his tight jeans, white shirt and blue shoes bend over her car was probably the only upside of the situation. Yet Bettie was starting to realise that they were going to be stuck here for a while and she hoped, prayed, whatever-ed that her mother's birthday cake wasn't going to spoil.

Granted it was cold enough. Late December was always cold in southeast England and all the little houses were covered in a thin layer of ice, frost and even a little snow, but Bettie didn't like how her breath condensed into long columns of vapour.

The smell of wonderfully warming spices filled the air and Bettie loved those smells as she remembered the buttery, luxurious mince pies she had eaten all over Christmas along with the fruity, boozy cake and yule logs. It really had been the perfect Christmas with her family and now she wanted to top it off with the perfect birthday for her mother, but that clearly wasn't going to happen within the next hour.

The sound of panicked voices in the distance made Bettie wonder what was going on. It was clear the voices were coming from further down the street, and considering Bettie had nothing better to do and Graham would never call the breakdown services, she had no other choice than to check out the sound.

And it meant Graham wouldn't be able to spring up the conversation of having kids on her again, like he had accidentally done that morning.

A conversation she really didn't want today. Especially as her mother was going to ask about it a thousand times already.

"Gra, I'm going down the street to check down

the sounds. Be back soon. Love you," Bettie said, walking down the street.

"Love you too Bet," Graham said.

Bettie actually looked at the houses as she went down the street, they were more beautiful than her quick glance had showed her earlier. Each house still had up their wide range of Christmas lights in all their different stunning colours. They were rather beautiful. Each one could probably be described as an art piece with how each house had shaped, decorated and sequenced their lights.

But why were the lights on at nine o'clock in the morning? It was hardly dark.

"The Gift is stolen!"

Bettie stared at the man who kept shouting the same thing over and over. She wasn't sure what to make of the man, he wasn't very tall, but his (hideously) bright Christmas jumper and trousers spoke volumes.

"Bettie English, Private Eye, can I help you?" she asked.

"Oh yes, you can," the man turned towards the rest of the street. "Everyone! The Great Give Away is saved!"

Bettie really didn't understand what was going on. At this rate she'll have to charge a confusion fee to these people.

As more and more people walked out of their houses towards Bettie, she couldn't believe how they all looked so different. Each person was a different height, weight and class. That alone was different from the rest of England.

"Miss? Who are you?" a little old lady said pulling on Bettie's arm.

Bettie introduced herself and wasn't sure what to make of the little old lady as her face lit up like a Christmas tree.

"Miss, the Great Give Away is lost without you?"

Now Bettie wished she had had that second mug of coffee like Graham had wanted her to. Damn him for being right!

"Sorry. What is the Great Give Away?" Bettie asked.

Everyone in the street gasped and looked at horror at Bettie.

"It's the most amazing time of the year!" everyone shouted.

The little old lady placed a cold hand on Bettie's shoulder.

"Miss. Every year on this day, we Give Away all our Christmas leftovers to the homeless so they may get fed through the New Year after our Christmas joy,"

That was a rather good idea actually, Bettie had never thought of that before. It made perfect sense and she was a bit surprised that no one else had thought of it. Everyone always bought too much at Christmas (that alone was disgusting) and everyone just threw it away (including her), but giving it to the homeless and less fortunate, now that was an excellent idea.

But the idea of someone stealing it was monstrous. Who in their right mind would steal from such a great idea?

It was probably as far from the Christmas spirit that you could get. Especially given the entire idea of St Nick and Father Christmas was to give the poor presents and help others. This theft was flat outrageous!

Bettie had to find out who did it.

The little old lady and everyone else grabbed Bettie and pulled her further down the street.

Bettie tried to resist but she just went along with it in the end.

Then the crowd pushed her in front of a large metal cage with red, pink and green tinsel covering it. But there was one very disturbing thing that caught Bettie's eyes, where a presumably large metal padlock should have been, there was only bend twisted metal.

"Is this where you stored the leftovers?" Bettie asked.

Another massive gasp from the crowd.

The little old lady gestured for the crowd to go away and leave her and Bettie alone.

"Miss. I'm sorry about that. For them The Great Give Away is the highlight of the year, they believe everyone should do it,"

"I do agree. Tell me what happened?"

"I run the street Miss. I own most of it and now walk up and down every morning and evening if my old body allows me. I walked past this morning to see the food was gone,"

"Was it there last night?" Bettie asked.

"Oh yes Miss. I bought some leftover... I mean The Gift of My Husband's Christmas Cake to donate,"

Bettie smiled. "It's okay. Say whatever you want to me, I won't get offended,"

"Thank you Miss,"

Bettie knelt down on the cold ground, looking at the twisted metal. It was clear that the lock had been forced off but that wasn't what bothered Bettie so much.

Now she was on the ground, Bettie saw stains of coffee, tea and syrups, but they were all going in the direction of the back of the cage. Not the front.

Bettie would have imagined if the thief had broken off the lock, then they would have pulled all the goods and leftovers through the front and presumably onto whatever they were using to transport the food away.

In fact the ground was cold, perfectly soft and perfectly intact. There were no impressions of feet or wheelbarrow marks or anything else that would suggest someone had been standing here weighted down with all the leftovers.

Something wasn't right here.

Bettie went round to the back of the metal cage.

"Here," Bettie said.

"What Miss?"

Bettie just pointed to the deep marks and the stains of tea, coffee and syrups in the mud.

"Oh Miss!" the little old lady said, her voice panicked.

Bettie tapped the back of the metal cage a few times and watched it vibrate, hum and eventually fall off.

"Someone must have carefully cut off the back part, stole the leftovers and twisted the lock off to make you think that was how the theft happened,"

"Oh dear Miss, oh dear. What will I do?"

Bettie stood up and placed a gentle hand on the old lady.

"Relax. It will be okay. I will find your leftovers for you. But can I ask a favour?"

"Anything Miss!"

Bettie smiled. "There's a little red car up the street with a hot man failing to fix my engine. Do you have a mechanic on the street please?"

Again the old lady's eyes lit up and she simply walked away.

Bettie had no idea if that meant they had a mechanic, or if the old lady had simply gone off to check out Graham. It sounded silly, but in Bettie's past experience the older women of the world did enjoy his looks. Thankfully she was younger than him by a few years.

Bettie knelt down next to the marks in the soft mud. They didn't look right or what she had seen from other thefts in her years as a private eye.

The marks were too narrow to be car wheels and she doubted anyone could get a car on the soft mud and get it off again without the car spinning out. Then again the marks were still too large to belong to a wheelbarrow.

And judging by the size of the metal cage and the odd marks of rice pudding on the top of it, Bettie was sure the cage had been stuffed full.

But the marks did go away from the metal cage towards one of the little houses who had a large brown fence.

Bettie went up to the fence and strangely enough the marks seemed to go straight under the fence like it wasn't there.

Maybe it hadn't?

Jumping out Bettie grabbed onto the top of the fence and pulled herself up, she'd forgotten how tough climbing was. In the new year she had to get back to the gym and do weight training, forget cardio, she had to do the weights!

Over the fence, Bettie didn't like the plainness of the little garden that she was looking at. All the garden had in it was a child's swing, a sandpit and a bed of half-dead flowers.

It all looked so plain and unloved. Unlike her garden, this one didn't scream love, nature or beauty. It looked like some half-ass attempt to make a garden fit for a family.

But the marks weren't in the garden.

"Can I help ya?" a woman said.

Bettie dropped down from the fence.

The woman in front of her was hardly a looker with her long twisted hair, short stocky body and black teeth, but Bettie had dealt with worse looking people.

"Yes actually. Did you-"

"Leave woman. I donna have time for ya. Go away and don't come back," the woman said starting to leave.

"Does your kid want a new bike?" Bettie said, randomly.

The woman stopped. "Go away. My kid don't want anything from a posh snob like you. Now leave,"

"How about some Gifts from The Great Give Away?"

The woman hissed at Bettie as she almost went into her house.

"Those snobs donna give me any. I might be poor, but I gotten a house. Now leave. I don't want ya charity,"

The door slammed shut and Bettie wasn't sure what to make of it. The woman was clearly annoyed at the street, snobs that lived here (even though Bettie had met snobs and these people weren't ones) and hated the Great Give Away.

But the woman had seen contempt at least a little bit to live her life how she wanted, Bettie doubted the woman wanted to do any harm to the world.

Bettie went over to the woman's door and pushed a twenty-pound note through the letterbox. At least the woman might be able to buy herself and her kids some food and maybe a nice treat with it.

The sound of a bike's bell made Bettie look at the street as she saw two young children ride around.

She still didn't know if she wanted kids, Graham definitely did, but he was a detective, she was a private eye. Full time jobs and lifestyles that didn't allow for kids, but she still had time to find out, if that's what she wanted.

Then Bettie looked at the tyres on the bikes, they were narrow, smaller than a car and wheelbarrow. They might be able to make the marks in the soft mud.

Bettie went over to the side of the road and knelt down.

"Kids," Bettie said, waving them over.

"Mum said don't talk to strangers!" one of the kids said, he was probably about ten.

Bettie rolled her eyes. "I'm a friend of the... little old lady, owns some of the houses,"

She had no idea if they would know who she was talking about.

"Mrs Birchwood!" the younger kid shouted, he was certainly six years old.

The ten year old kid got off his bike and walked over to Bettie, keeping at least three metres between himself and her. Very clever, Bettie was going to have to remember that if she had kids. Three metres was more than enough space to run away if she wanted to kidnap him.

Of course she didn't, but still.

"Are you two the only ones with bikes in the street?" Bettie asked.

"Na. Jonny boy has a big bikey for big boys,"

"Has he ride a lot?"

"Ya. Saw him riding last night after Birchwood did her walky. I donna think she was gotten make it back home, I was gonna ride her home but mum said no,"

Bettie only just realised that there was something amazing about young children. They always wanted to love, help and support others no matter what, if she was going to have kids, she had to teach them that. And then make sure they didn't lose it when they grew up.

"That's very good of you. Well done. Now where do I find this Jonny Boy?"

The kid shrugged, jumped on his bike and they both rode off again.

***

When Bettie returned to her little red car she was expecting to stare at her beautiful Graham bent over the engine failing to fix it. Instead she found the little old lady bend over and hammering away at the engine.

The wonderful smell of the warming Christmas spices filled the air as Bettie went up to Graham who had a few dark smudges on his white shirt and tight jeans, but he was still the sexy, most beautiful man Bettie had ever seen.

"At least you tried," Bettie said, rubbing

Graham's muscular shoulder.

"You clearly didn't trust me," Graham said, pretending to hit her cheek.

The little old lady climbed down to the ground and out of the car and turned to Bettie.

"Miss, your car should be working again in no time. Cars advanced a lot since the war but it will work,"

"You worked in the war?" Bettie asked, doubting the old lady was old enough to serve during World War Two.

"Oh no Miss, me dad served and I was born later. He taught me a lot about cars, trucks and planes from the war. I was quite the fixer in the neighbourhood. Have you found the Great Give Away?"

"The Great Give Away?" Graham asked.

Bettie just waved Graham silent.

"That's why I came to find you. One, thank you for your father's service. Two, who is Jonny Boy?"

The Little Old Lady shrugged.

"I met two kids who called him that and said he had a bike for big boys. Maybe he's an older kid or a young adult?" Bettie said.

"Oh! Miss, you mean Jonathan Bodie,"

Now Bettie shrugged. She didn't know anyone on the street, and yet this woman was acting like Bettie was a local.

"Um yes. Where is he?" Bettie asked.

The little old lady started to walk down the street.

"Come on Miss English. I'm waiting for a part from my garage. My Husband will find it soon. I'll show you where he lives,"

Bettie gestured Graham to follow and they both

followed the little old lady down the street. Even with the sun high in the sky, Bettie couldn't believe how cold and dark it was, but that was the strange thing about English weather, it never seemed natural.

The days were meant to get brighter after the Winter Solstice but they seemed to be getting darker and darker and darker, and even at ten O'clock it wasn't what Bettie would call bright.

But the strangeness of the English weather was something she loved about it though.

After a few more minutes of walking down the street, the little old lady pointed to a bright red and green door with a large wreath on it.

Bettie went up to it and knocked three times.

"Mr Bodie," Bettie said.

A tall man opened the door and Bettie was immediately taken by the amount of aftershave he was wearing, she had to focus on not passing out of its strength. It wasn't even a nice aftershave, not like the earthy, sexy one Graham was wearing.

"Merry Christmas!" Jonathan Bodie said in a happy manly voice.

"Um, Happy Christmas. Did you ride your bike last night?" Bettie asked.

She wanted to start off easy and at least place him at the scene of the crime before outright accusing him. Yet the man seemed too happy and filled with the Christmas spirit to want to steal and ruin the Christmas Season for others.

"Oh Yes, I love cycling. It's wonderful. Especially seeing all the amazing lights. Have you seen them! Have you seen them!"

Bettie nodded. "They are wonderful. Did you go to the Give Away… cage last night?"

Bodie's expression changed to a solid frown and his eyes flicked towards Graham.

Bettie clicked her fingers at him. "Yes he is a cop. But I'm not. Confess to me and nothing can happen to you. I won't tell him, you have my word,"

Bodie's eyes flicked between Bettie and Graham and a few times at the little old lady.

"The homeless peeps can't have the food. We need it. Well, my daughter's charity needs it,"

Bettie shook her head. "You're telling me. You stole the food for the good of others?"

Bodie's eyes widened and he frantically nodded.

Bettie looked at Graham and the little old lady.

"We're going to need a cup of tea for this one," she said.

"Bodie, let the Miss and Graham come in," the little old lady said.

Bettie looked at Bodie who slowly nodded his head and stepped out of the way.

***

The living room of Bodie's house was a lot nicer than Bettie had imagined. She loved his bright blue three seat sofa, chair opposite it and coffee table in the middle.

The living room was definitely small and minimalist but Bodie had managed to make it comforting and cozy and rather lovely despite its size.

There were a few pictures of his wife and presumably his three children on the walls and seeing all those pictures and the happiness of the family made Bettie just stare at Graham.

He was happy, sexy and beautiful, a perfect man who would make an amazing dad. Then she would make a great mother she supposed, Bettie loved her nephew Sean like her own child and had raised him (sometimes) a lot more than his own parents.

So maybe she could have children.

"Please sit down," Bodie said gesturing towards the three seat sofa as he sat down on the chair opposite them.

Bettie sat down. "Your daughter works for a charity?"

Bodie looked at the little old lady. "I'm sorry Margaret. I didn't mean to steal it. My daughter... my daughter just wanted a little help,"

"It's fine deary. But why didn't you just ask?"

Bodie looked to the ground. "I was embarrassed,"

"What is the charity?" Bettie asked.

"It's brilliant Miss. I love it. It's a new charity that helps the homeless, vulnerable youths and even the elderly,"

"My daughter wanted a little help. I didn't want the Great Give Away to only go to one type of person," Bodie said.

Bettie could agree with that. Her nephew could have been one of the vulnerable youths if her (idiot) of a brother-in-law had kicked him out when her nephew said he was gay. Sure Sean would have been homeless but he was still a vulnerable youth, it wasn't fair that he wouldn't necessarily benefit from the Great Give Away, just because he was young.

And most homeless in the area were older.

Bettie leant forward. "Graham I don't think there's a crime here if we reach an agreement,"

Graham smiled and Bettie loved that sexy movie star smile.

"Me either Bet, but what sort of agreement?"

Graham said.

"Well why don't you Mr Bodie and… Margaret agree to support your daughter's charity with the Great Give Away so she can help even more people?"

Both Bodie and Margaret looked at each other and smiled.

"Oh Miss that is a wonderful idea. That way we can all help the homeless, young and the elderly! That is marvellous!"

Bodie nodded too and judging by his face he was trying to hold back some tears.

Bettie stood up and looked at Bodie. "Just to check I presume the food is all in the garage safe and sound,"

Bodie nodded.

"Good. We will leave you both to sort out the details," Bettie said with a smile.

Graham started to head out the door and Bettie went to follow him when Margaret grabbed her arm.

"Thank you Miss! Thank you. You've saved the Great Give Away. What do I owe you?"

Judging by the look on Graham's face as he looked outside, her car was fixed and there was something wonderful about the little street.

Unlike the normal streets of southeast England, this one actually had soul, character and love in it. All these people no matter their background all loved each other in their own unique ways and wanted to help others. Hence the Great Give Away, Bettie wasn't going to charge people who wanted to help out others and help make the world a better place.

"Nothing," Bettie said smiling and walking out of the house. "Merry Great Give Away and A Happy New Year,"

Bettie heard Margaret and Bodie laugh, talk and being happy as she left, and her and Graham walked back up the street towards her car that was working perfectly.

There was a little old man walking away covered in oil and black smudges. He had to be Margaret's husband and the one who fixed the car properly.

She really wished everyone on the street, in England and the rest of the world had a great day and in some small way benefited from the Great Give Away. Because for some reason, a reason even Bettie didn't understand, she truly believed that every little act of kindness helped to make the world a better place.

Bettie wrapped her arm around Graham's waist and buried her face into his shoulder.

"When we get home tonight, we're so doing two things," Bettie said.

"What?"

"We're going to empty the house of the leftovers and take it down to the food bank,"

Graham smile and nodded at that.

Bettie stopped and pulled Graham close. "And we're going to make a baby,"

Graham's face lit up, they kissed and Bettie loved the soft feeling of his lips.

"Merry Great Give Away Bet,"

As Bettie pressed her lips against his, the entire world felt right as she had saved a made-up holiday for people, helped a charity and now she was going to be something she never thought she had wanted.

A mother.

And she had done that all before Eleven O'clock in the morning. A great, brilliant, perfect start to an amazing day.

MADE-UP HOLIDAYS COLLECTION

GET YOUR FREE AND EXCLUSIVE SHORT STORY NOW! LEARN ABOUT NEMESIO'S PAST!

https://www.subscribepage.com/fireheart

About the author:

Connor Whiteley is the author of over 60 books in the sci-fi fantasy, nonfiction psychology and books for writer's genre and he is a Human Branding Speaker and Consultant.

He is a passionate warhammer 40,000 reader, psychology student and author.

Who narrates his own audiobooks and he hosts The Psychology World Podcast.

All whilst studying Psychology at the University of Kent, England.

Also, he was a former Explorer Scout where he gave a speech to the Maltese President in August 2018 and he attended Prince Charles' 70th Birthday Party at Buckingham Palace in May 2018.

Plus, he is a self-confessed coffee lover!

MADE-UP HOLIDAYS COLLECTION

<u>More From The Holiday Extravaganza:</u>
<u>Criminal Christmas:</u>
Crime, Christmas, Closet
Protecting Christmas
Christmas Thief
Christmas, Crime, letter
Private Eye, Convention and Christmas
Cheater At Dinner
Perfect Christmas
Salvation In The Maid
Criminal, Resistance, Alliance
Dark Farm
Great Give Away

<u>Sweet Christmas</u>
Lights, Love, Christmas
Journalist, Zookeeper, Love
Young Romantic Hearts
Love In The Newspaper
Holiday, Burnout, Love
Homeless, Charity, Love
Cold December Night
Driving Home For Love
Love At The Winter Wedding
Fireworks, New Year, Love
Loving In The New Year Tourist

<u>Fantastical Christmas:</u>
Magic That Binds
One Final Christmas
Author's Christmas Problems
Last Winter Dragon Egg
A Sacrifice For Saturnalia
Soulcaster
Weird First Christmas
All Feast
Solstice Guardian
Wheel of Years
Repent

MADE-UP HOLIDAYS COLLECTION

OTHER SHORT STORIES BY CONNOR WHITELEY

Mystery Short Stories:
Poison In The Candy Cane
Christmas Innocence
You Better Watch Out
Christmas Theft
Trouble In Christmas
Smell of The Lake
Problem In A Car
Theft, Past and Team
Embezzler In The Room
A Strange Way To Go
A Horrible Way To Go
Ann Awful Way To Go
An Old Way To Go
A Fishy Way To Go
A Pointy Way To Go
A High Way To Go
A Fiery Way To Go
A Glassy Way To Go
A Chocolatey Way To Go
Kendra Detective Mystery Collection Volume 1
Kendra Detective Mystery Collection Volume 2
Stealing A Chance At Freedom

Glassblowing and Death
Theft of Independence
Cookie Thief
Marble Thief
Book Thief
Art Thief
Mated At The Morgue
The Big Five Whoopee Moments
Stealing An Election
Mystery Short Story Collection Volume 1
Mystery Short Story Collection Volume 2

Science Fiction Short Stories:
The First Rememberer
Life of A Rememberer
System of Wonder
Lifesaver
Remarkable Way She Died
The Interrogation of Annabella Stormic
Blade of The Emperor
Arbiter's Truth
Computation of Battle
Old One's Wrath
Puppets and Masters
Ship of Plague
Interrogation
Edge of Failure

MADE-UP HOLIDAYS COLLECTION

One Way Choice
Acceptable Losses
Balance of Power
Good Idea At The Time
Escape Plan
Escape In The Hesitation
Inspiration In Need
Singing Warriors
Knowledge is Power
Killer of Polluters
Climate of Death
The Family Mailing Affair
Defining Criminality
The Martian Affair
A Cheating Affair
The Little Café Affair
Mountain of Death
Prisoner's Fight
Claws of Death
Bitter Air
Honey Hunt
Blade On A Train

<u>Fantasy Short Stories:</u>
City of Snow
City of Light
City of Vengeance
Dragons, Goats and Kingdom
Smog The Pathetic Dragon
Don't Go In The Shed
The Tomato Saver
The Remarkable Way She Died
The Bloodied Rose
Asmodia's Wrath
Heart of A Killer
Emissary of Blood
Dragon Coins
Dragon Tea
Dragon Rider
Sacrifice of the Soul
Heart of The Flesheater
Heart of The Regent
Heart of The Standing
Feline of The Lost
Heart of The Story
City of Fire
Awaiting Death

Other books by Connor Whiteley:

Bettie English Private Eye Series
A Very Private Woman
The Russian Case
A Very Urgent Matter
A Case Most Personal
Trains, Scots and Private Eyes
The Federation Protects

The Fireheart Fantasy Series
Heart of Fire
Heart of Lies
Heart of Prophecy
Heart of Bones
Heart of Fate

City of Assassins (Urban Fantasy)
City of Death
City of Marytrs
City of Pleasure
City of Power

Agents of The Emperor
Return of The Ancient Ones
Vigilance
Angels of Fire
Kingmaker

The Garro Series- Fantasy/Sci-fi
GARRO: GALAXY'S END
GARRO: RISE OF THE ORDER
GARRO: END TIMES
GARRO: SHORT STORIES
GARRO: COLLECTION
GARRO: HERESY
GARRO: FAITHLESS
GARRO: DESTROYER OF WORLDS
GARRO: COLLECTIONS BOOK 4-6
GARRO: MISTRESS OF BLOOD
GARRO: BEACON OF HOPE
GARRO: END OF DAYS

Winter Series- Fantasy Trilogy Books
WINTER'S COMING
WINTER'S HUNT
WINTER'S REVENGE
WINTER'S DISSENSION

Miscellaneous:
RETURN
FREEDOM
SALVATION
Reflection of Mount Flame
The Masked One
The Great Deer

www.ingramcontent.com/pod-product-compliance
Lightning Source LLC
LaVergne TN
LVHW011843060526
838200LV00054B/4143